Sadie's Lag Ba'Omer Mystery

For my dad, Bob Korngold the poet, who told the stories and passed the torch. —J.K.

For Don, with love—J.F.

Kar-Ben Publishing
An imprint of Lerner Publishing Group, Inc.
241 First Avenue North
Minneapolis, MN 55401 U.S.A.

Website address: www.karben.com

Library of Congress Cataloging-in-Publication Data

Korngold, Jamie S.
  Sadie's Lag Ba'Omer mystery / by Jamie Korngold ; illustrated by Julie Fortenberry.
    p.   cm.
    Summary: "Sadie and her brother Ori want to learn about the Jewish holiday Lag Ba'Omer"—Provided by publisher.
    ISBN 978-0-7613-9047-3 (lib. bdg. : alk. paper)
    [1. Lag b'Omer—Fiction. 2. Judaism—Customs and practices—Fiction. 3. Brothers and sisters—Fiction. 4. Jews—United States—Fiction.] I. Fortenberry, Julie, 1956- illustrator. II. Title.
  PZ7.K83749Sacs 2014
  [E]—dc23   2013002189

Manufactured in China
2-51523-16971-7/30/2021

0422/B507/A6

Sadie's Lag Ba'Omer Mystery

By Jamie Korngold

illustrated by Julie Fortenberry

KAR-BEN
PUBLISHING

One warm spring night,

Sadie and Ori were out walking with their grandpa, when they saw the full moon rise over the treetops. Startled by its brightness, Sadie asked, "What holiday is it?" At Hebrew school she had learned that Jewish holidays often begin with a full moon.

"The last full moon was on Passover, and the full moon before that was on Purim," Ori remembered.

"But what holiday comes this month?"

"Ahhh!" said Grandpa, "there is no holiday on the full moon this month, but there is a holiday soon after. Can you guess what it is?"

Sadie looked at Ori.

Ori looked at Sadie.

"It's a mystery!" they said together.

"Jewish history has many mysteries," Grandpa agreed.

The next day, Sadie and Ori started to work on the mystery. Sadie looked on her calendar. A few days past the big circle showing the full moon, she read: **Lag Ba'Omer.**

"What's Lag Ba' Omer?" asked Ori.

Sadie looked at Ori.

Ori looked at Sadie.

"It's a mystery!" they said together.

First they looked on their bookshelves.

Sadie found books about Rosh Hashanah and Yom Kippur.

Ori found books about Sukkot and Simchat Torah.

Sadie found books about Hanukkah and Purim.

Ori found books about Passover and Shavuot.

But neither one found a single book about Lag Ba'Omer.

In the living room, Ori found the shofar their father blew on Rosh Hashanah and Yom Kippur.

Sadie found the little Torah she carried on Simchat Torah.

Ori found menorahs and dreidels for Hanukkah.

Sadie found candlesticks and Kiddush cups for Shabbat.

But they didn't find anything for Lag Ba'Omer.

"We need to ask some holiday experts," Sadie said.

She asked the delivery man. "What kind of presents do you deliver for Lag Ba'Omer?"

"I don't think I deliver presents for Lag Ba'Omer," he said. "What is Lag Ba'Omer?"

Ori asked Aunt Katy.
"What do you do on Lag Ba'Omer?"

"Isn't that when you go on picnics?"
she suggested.

Sadie asked Uncle Danny.
"What songs do you sing on Lag Ba'Omer?"

"Isn't that the holiday with bonfires?
I guess you would sing campfire songs."

Ori asked Grandma.
"What do you cook on Lag Ba'Omer?"

"You cook delicious foods, like you do on
every Jewish holiday," Grandma answered.

Sadie and Ori found Grandpa outside, reading on the porch swing.

"Did you solve the mystery?" he asked.

"We've discovered that you go on picnics, build bonfires, sing songs, and eat delicious food," announced Ori.

"Sounds like a good holiday to me," said Grandpa.

"But Grandpa," Sadie asked. "What IS Lag Ba'Omer?"

Grandpa closed his book, helped his grandchildren climb up beside him on the swing, and began:

A long time ago, there lived a great and wise teacher named Rabbi Shimon Bar Yochai. Children came from far and wide to study with him. But the Roman emperor decreed that Jews could no longer study Torah. Rabbi Shimon was very sad. He missed teaching the children. At first the students were happy to have time to play. But soon they missed their teacher and his clever stories. They knew they had to figure out a way to continue to study and learn.

One day, while running in the woods, the children found a secret cave hidden behind some trees. Inside, they discovered a huge room, with a stream large enough to splash in. They showed it to Rabbi Shimon. He agreed it was the perfect hiding spot for him to study and for them to come and learn.

The cave became Rabbi Shimon's home. He drank water from its spring, and ate the fruit of the carob tree that grew at its entrance.

And the cave became a classroom where students studied Torah with Rabbi Shimon. To fool the Romans, the children often packed picnics, as if they were going off on an outing. Some disguised themselves as hunters and carried bows and arrows.

Rabbi Shimon lived in the cave for many years, until the Roman emperor died, and the decree was lifted.

Lag Ba'Omer has become a day to remember Rabbi Shimon. Jews all over the world gather around bonfires to have picnics, sing, dance, and tell stories about his bravery.

"This year, let's build our own bonfire,"
Ori said, when Grandpa had finished.
"We can invite our friends to celebrate."

On Lag Ba'Omer, Sadie and Ori, and their family and friends, gathered in their backyard. The picnic table was piled high with corn on the cob, grilled chicken legs, crisp green salad, chocolate brownies, and strawberry lemonade.

After dinner, they lit a bonfire. Sadie and Ori's mother reached for her guitar and began to play. Soon everyone joined in singing.

"We've solved the mystery of Lag Ba'Omer!" Sadie told Ori, as sparks from the campfire lit the sky.

Lag Ba'Omer

Lag Ba'Omer is the 33rd day of the Omer*, the period between the holidays of Passover and Shavuot. The omer was a measure of grain that was brought to the Temple on the second day of Passover, and the Torah commands us to count seven weeks, and to celebrate a new holiday (Shavuot) when the counting is completed. The rabbis say this shows that the giving of Torah on Shavuot is the culmination of the Exodus from Egypt. Varied explanations are given for the designation of Lag Ba'Omer as a holiday, a minor one in the Jewish calendar. Traditionally, it marks both the birth and death of Rabbi Shimon Bar Yochai, the author of the mystical Zohar. In Israel celebrations take place at his gravesite in Meron. The Omer is also a period of mourning for the thousands of students of Rabbi Akiva who died in a plague during the 2nd century. During the Omer weddings and musical entertainment are prohibited, and many refrain from haircuts. According to tradition, the plague stopped on Lag Ba'Omer, and thus the day has become a time for weddings, as well as first haircuts for little boys.

*According to numerical values assigned to Hebrew letters, lamed is 30; gimmel is 3. "Lag" is an abbreviation for "Lamed Gimmel."

About the Author

Rabbi Jamie S. Korngold, who received ordination from the Hebrew Union College-Jewish Institute of Religion, is the founder and spiritual leader of The Adventure Rabbi: Synagogue Without Walls. She has competed in ultra-marathons, national ski competitions, and rode her bike across the U.S. at age 16. She has worked as a street musician in Japan and as a cook on a boat in Alaska. Rabbi Korngold is the author of "Sadie's Sukkah Breakfast," "Sadie and the Big Mountain," "Sadie's Almost Marvelous Menorah," (Kar-Ben), "God in the Wilderness" (Doubleday), and "The God Upgrade" (Jewish Lights). She lives in Boulder, Colorado with her husband and two daughters.

About the Illustrator

Julie Fortenberry is an abstract painter and a children's book illustrator. She has a Master's Degree in Fine Arts from Hunter College in New York. Her children's books include "Sadie's Sukkah Breakfast," "Sadie and the Big Mountain," "Sadie's Almost Marvelous Menorah," (Kar-Ben) and "Pippa at the Parade" (Boyds Mills Press). She lives in Chatham County, North Carolina.